I am the world

Dedicated to all children of the world.

—C. R. S. Jr.

A
atheneum

ATHENEUM BOOKS FOR YOUNG READERS
An imprint of Simon & Schuster Children's Publishing Division
1230 Avenue of the Americas, New York, New York 10020
Copyright © 2013 by Charles R. Smith Jr.
All rights reserved, including the right of reproduction in whole or in part in any form.
ATHENEUM BOOKS FOR YOUNG READERS is a registered trademark of Simon & Schuster, Inc.
Atheneum logo is a trademark of Simon & Schuster, Inc.
For information about special discounts for bulk purchases, please contact Simon & Schuster Special Sales at 1-866-506-1949 or
business@simonandschuster.com.
The Simon & Schuster Speakers Bureau can bring authors to your live event. For more information or to book an event, contact the
Simon & Schuster Speakers Bureau at 1-866-248-3049 or visit our website at www.simonspeakers.com.
Book design by Sonia Chaghatzbanian
The text for this book is set in Neutraface.
The photographs for this book are rendered digitally.
Manufactured in China
0413 SCP
First Edition
2 4 6 8 10 9 7 5 3 1
CIP data for this book is available from the Library of Congress.
ISBN 978-1-4424-2302-2
ISBN 978-1-4424-8295-1 (eBook)

I am the world

Charles R. Smith Jr.

Atheneum Books for Young Readers
NEW YORK LONDON TORONTO SYDNEY NEW DELHI

I am the world.

I am strong.

I am the spirit of generations gone.

I am the blood of emperors.

I am the
wisdom of queens.

I am the

heart **of warriors.**

I am the soul of kings.

I am
the honor
of Asia.

I am the
smile
of Irish
pride.

I am the breeze
of islands

far and wide.

I am
the bite
in bratwurst.

I am the fire
in wasabi.

I am the thread in kente cloth.

I am the pleat in Highland kilts.

I am the history in Indian ghagras.

I am a stitch of Chinese

silk.

I am the rhythm in capoeira.

I am the roots of calypso.

I am the clickety-clack-clack of castanets in flamenco.

I am
hello, jambo, bonjour, zdravo.

Namaste, ni hao, hola, buon giorno.

I am a fiber in the flag

of humanity.

I am the world

and the world is **me.**

Glossary

Biscotti (bis-cot-ti): small, crisp, rectangular, twice-baked cookies typically containing nuts. Originally from Italy.

Bonjour (bon-jour): "Hello" or "Good day" in French.

Bratwurst (brat-wurst): a type of fine German pork sausage that is either fried or grilled.

Buon giorno (bone gior-no): "Hello" or "Good day" in Italian.

Calypso (ca-lip-so): a style of Caribbean music that originated in Trinidad and Tobago.

Capoeira (ca-po-ei-ra): a combination of martial arts, dance, and music originally created by slaves in Brazil.

Castanets (cas-ta-nets): small pieces of wood, ivory, or plastic joined in pairs by a piece of cord and clicked together by the fingers in Spanish dancing.

Emperor (em-per-or): ruler of an empire.

Flamenco (fla-men-co): a style of Spanish music played especially on the guitar and accompanied by singing and dancing.

Ghagras (gha-gra): a traditional dress worn by girls of North India.

Hola (o-la): "Hello" in Spanish.

Jambo (jam-bo): "Hello" in Swahili, a language of Africa.

Kente (ken-te): a brightly colored, patterned material from Ghana, Africa.

Kilt (kilt): a knee-length skirt of pleated tartan cloth traditionally worn by men as part of Scottish Highland dress.

Namaste (na-ma-ste): traditional greeting from India.

Ni hao (nee-how): "Hello" in Mandarin Chinese.

Pierogi (pi-ro-gi): a semicircular dumpling with any variety of fillings, such as chopped meat or vegetables. Originally from Poland.

Silk (silk): a fine, strong, soft, fiber produced by silkworms.

Warrior (war-rior): a brave or experienced soldier or fighter.

Wasabi (wa-sa-bi): a Japanese plant with a thick green root used in cooking, usually as a powder or paste; served with sushi.

Zdravo (str-avo): "Hello" in Serbo-Croatian.

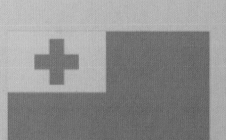
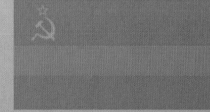

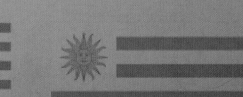